This book belongs to

_____

Thumbelina

BY

Hans Christian Andersen

Retold by Jennifer Greenway

ILLUSTRATED BY

Robyn Officer

ARIEL BOOKS

ANDREWS AND McMEEL

KANSAS CITY

Library of Congress Cataloging-in-Publication Data

Andersen, H. C. (Hans Christian), 1805–1875.
    [Tommelise. English]
    Thumbelina / by Hans Christian Andersen ; illustrated by
Robyn Officer.
       p.   cm.
    Summary: After being kidnapped by an ugly toad, a beautiful girl no bigger than a thumb has a series of dreadful experiences before meeting a fairy prince just her size.
    ISBN 0-8362-4926-7 : $6.95
    [1. Fairy tales.] I. Officer, Robyn, ill. II. Title.
PZ8.A542Th   1991b
[E]—dc20   91–30045
                                              CIP
                                              AC

Design: Susan Hood and Mike Hortens
Art Direction: Armand Eisen, Mike Hortens, and Julie Phillips
Art Production: Lynn Wine
Production: Julie Miller and Lisa Shadid

Thumbelina

$\mathcal{T}$here once lived a couple who longed to have a child, but their wish did not come true. At last, the woman went to a fairy and asked for her help. The fairy gave her a seed and said, "Plant this in a flowerpot and water it carefully."

Soon a beautiful flower sprang up. It looked like a tulip with its petals tightly closed.

"How lovely," said the woman, kissing the flower. As she did so, the petals opened. Inside sat a tiny, graceful girl no bigger than the woman's thumb. The woman was overjoyed. She and her husband named the child Thumbelina.

Thumbelina's cradle was a walnut shell. She had a pillow of violets and a quilt of rose petals. At night her cradle sat on the windowsill. During the day, the woman kept a bowl filled with water on the table. Thumbelina amused herself by rowing around the bowl in a boat made of a large tulip petal. She used two white horsehairs for oars. As she rowed, she sang in the tiniest, prettiest voice imaginable.

One night a big ugly toad hopped through the window. When the toad saw Thumbelina asleep in her cradle, she cried, "She would make the perfect wife for my son!"

The ugly toad snatched the cradle with Thumbelina inside and carried it to her home in the swamp.

The toad set Thumbelina on a large lily pad in the middle of the water so she could not escape. Then she went to fetch her son, who was even bigger and uglier than she was.

While the toad was gone, Thumbelina woke up. When she saw where she was, she began to cry and wonder how she would ever get home again. Some fish swimming below heard Thumbelina's cries.

When the fish saw how pretty Thumbelina was, they felt sorry for her. "We must set her free," they said, "so she does not have to marry the toad's son." The little fish began to bite at the stem of the lily pad. Before

long, they had gnawed through it, and the lily pad floated away.

Just then the toad returned with her son. "Stop!" the son called after Thumbelina. "Where are you going? You are to be my wife and live with me here in the swamp!" But it was too late. Thumbelina was already floating downstream.

Thumbelina went a long way, past wide green fields and deep shady woods. Birds and butterflies stopped to say hello to her, and she felt very happy.

Suddenly, a big brown beetle swooped down and seized Thumbelina in his claws. "How pretty you are!" he said. "I shall make you my wife!" How frightened Thumbelina was, but there was nothing she could do!

The beetle sat her on the branch of a tall
tree to show her to the other beetles. But
they did not think Thumbelina was pretty at
all. "How ugly she is!" they sneered, turning
up their feelers. "Her waist is so slim, and
she has only two legs! She looks horrible!"

After that, the beetle decided he didn't
want Thumbelina for a wife after all. So he
flew her down from the tree and set her on a
daisy.

Thumbelina was very sad, since she felt the beetles were right. She did not know that she was really very lovely.

All summer Thumbelina lived in the forest. She wove herself a bed of grass and hung it under a large leaf to shelter herself from the rain. She drank the morning dew and ate nectar from the flowers. She was perfectly content until autumn came—and then winter.

First, the leaf Thumbelina lived under died and shriveled. Now she had no shelter from the wind and rain. There was no longer any food to eat, either. Then it began to snow, and Thumbelina almost froze to death. So she went looking for food and shelter.

She walked until she came to a large cornfield. The cornstalks had been cut long before. Nothing was left but the stubble, which to Thumbelina seemed as tall as a great forest. At last, she found the home of a field mouse.

She knocked timidly on the door. When the field mouse answered, Thumbelina said shyly, "Please, can you spare a grain of barley?"

The field mouse, who was a kind thing, replied, "Of course! Come in, you dear little creature!" She led Thumbelina inside and fed her.

The field mouse's home was very comfortable, and her cupboards were full of the food she had stored for winter. So she told Thumbelina, "If you will keep my house tidy for me and tell me some good stories, you may stay with me all winter, if you like."

"Yes, please!" cried Thumbelina. And so she did all that the field mouse asked, and in return she was kept warm and well-fed.

One day the field mouse said, "Listen, Thumbelina. My neighbor is coming to pay us a visit tomorrow. He is much richer than I, and he wears a beautiful black velvet coat. Oh, he is a very clever man! But he is blind, so be sure to tell him your very best stories."

"Of course," said Thumbelina. But she was not very excited about the visitor, for he was a mole.

The mole came the next day, wearing his black velvet coat. Even though he was very rich and probably very learned, as well, Thumbelina did not like him. He said dreadful things about the sun and the flowers and birds, yet he had never seen them.

20

Nevertheless, Thumbelina told him her best stories and sang him all the songs she knew. She had such a lovely voice that the mole fell in love with her. However, he did not say anything, because he was very cautious. Instead, he invited Thumbelina and the field mouse to pay him a visit.

So the three set out through a tunnel the mole had recently dug between his home and that of the field mouse. "Now, please watch your step," the mole told them. "It's quite dark here and there is a dead bird farther down the tunnel. But don't let that alarm you!"

When they came to the dead bird, the mole accidentally pushed his nose through the roof of the tunnel. The sun came shining through, and Thumbelina clearly saw the bird.

He was a swallow, and he did not look as if he had been dead for long. "Poor bird," Thumbelina thought sadly. "He must have died of the cold."

The mole pushed the bird aside roughly. "Useless creatures, birds!" he said gruffly. Thumbelina said nothing. But when the mole and the field mouse had gone ahead, she bent over and kissed the bird. "Perhaps you were one of the birds that sang to me all summer," she said. "How nice it was to hear your sweet music!"

After the mole showed them his house and gave them tea, he led them home again. Then he repaired the hole so no sunlight or

cold could enter. But that night Thumbelina could not sleep.

She kept thinking of the poor swallow in the tunnel. At last, she crept from her bed and wove a blanket out of hay. She took it into the tunnel and laid it gently over the swallow.

Thumbelina sadly laid her head on the bird's breast. When she did, she heard a sound. It was the beating of the swallow's heart. He was not dead, only numb with cold. Thumbelina was afraid—the swallow was much bigger than she—but she bravely wrapped the blanket more tightly around him. Then she tiptoed away.

The next day she slipped away to visit the swallow again. He was awake now but very weak. So Thumbelina brought him water and honey, and all through the long cold winter she carefully nursed the swallow back to health. She told the field mouse and the

mole nothing of this, for they did not think much of birds.

At last, spring came. The swallow was now well enough to fly away. Thumbelina re-opened the hole in the roof of the tunnel for him.

"Why don't you come with me?" the swallow asked Thumbelina. "I can take you to warm, beautiful places."

Thumbelina dearly wished she could go with the swallow, but she shook her head.

"The field mouse has been very kind to me," she said, "I cannot just leave her!"

"Very well," said the swallow. "Farewell, kind maiden. I hope I see you again." And with that, the swallow flew away.

Tears filled Thumbelina's eyes. She was very fond of the swallow and would miss him so much.

Spring passed, then summer. Thumbelina worked for the field mouse, who treated her kindly but hardly ever let her go outside into the beautiful sunshine.

One day, as autumn was coming, the field mouse said to her, "I have good news, dear Thumbelina. The mole has asked for your hand in marriage. We must work to get your wedding clothes ready!"

"But I don't want to marry the mole!" cried Thumbelina, bursting into tears at the thought of living with him in his dark, underground tunnel far from the bright sun and all the lovely flowers.

"Don't be silly," the field mouse said crossly. "The mole is handsome and rich. He will make you an excellent husband. Marry him or I will bite you!"

The field mouse told Thumbelina the wedding would take place in a month. Four spiders spun the wedding veil, while Thumbelina sewed her tiny wedding gown.

As the wedding day drew near, Thumbelina became sadder and sadder. How dreadful it would be to always live in the darkness. Would she ever see the blue sky or the bright sun again? Would she ever hear a bird sing?

The day before the wedding, Thumbelina begged the field mouse to let her go outside one last time. At last, the field mouse gave her permission.

Thumbelina slipped out the door and stared longingly at the bright sky.

"Farewell, beautiful sun," she cried, stretching out her arms. "Farewell, sweet flowers! Please say hello to my dear swallow for me if you ever see him again!"

Just then Thumbelina heard a tweet, tweet above her head, and there was the swallow himself! He was flying south for winter, and he had come to say good-bye to Thumbelina before he went.

Thumbelina began to cry. She told him how she was to marry the mole the next day.

"Oh, no," cried the swallow. "Come with me instead. I will fly you to beautiful lands where the sun always shines and flowers always bloom."

"Oh, yes," Thumbelina said, "I will go with you!" for she could not bear to marry the mole.

Quickly she climbed on the swallow's back. Then the bird spread his wings and he and Thumbelina flew away. They flew over tall pine forests and snow-covered mountain peaks to warm countries where the grass is always green and orange and lemon trees grow.

After several days, they came to a clear blue lake. An ancient palace of white marble stood beside it. In the garden lay a marble pillar broken into three pieces.

Large, beautiful flowers were growing among the pieces of pillar. The swallow placed Thumbelina beside the most beautiful flower. "I think you will be happy here," he told her.

Just then the petals opened. Inside was a tiny man with shining gossamer wings. He

was the fairy of that flower and king of all the flower fairies. He was just Thumbelina's size, and he fell in love with her at once.

"Will you be my wife?" he asked. Thumbelina smiled, for he was nothing like the horrible mole. "Yes," she said happily.

At that all the flowers opened and each flower fairy gave Thumbelina a gift. The best gift of all was a pair of tiny gossamer wings. Now Thumbelina would be able to fly and flit from flower to flower.

At Thumbelina's wedding to the fairy king, the swallow sang a special wedding song. Then it was time for him to fly back north. As he went he sang of Thumbelina, and that is how we came to hear her story.